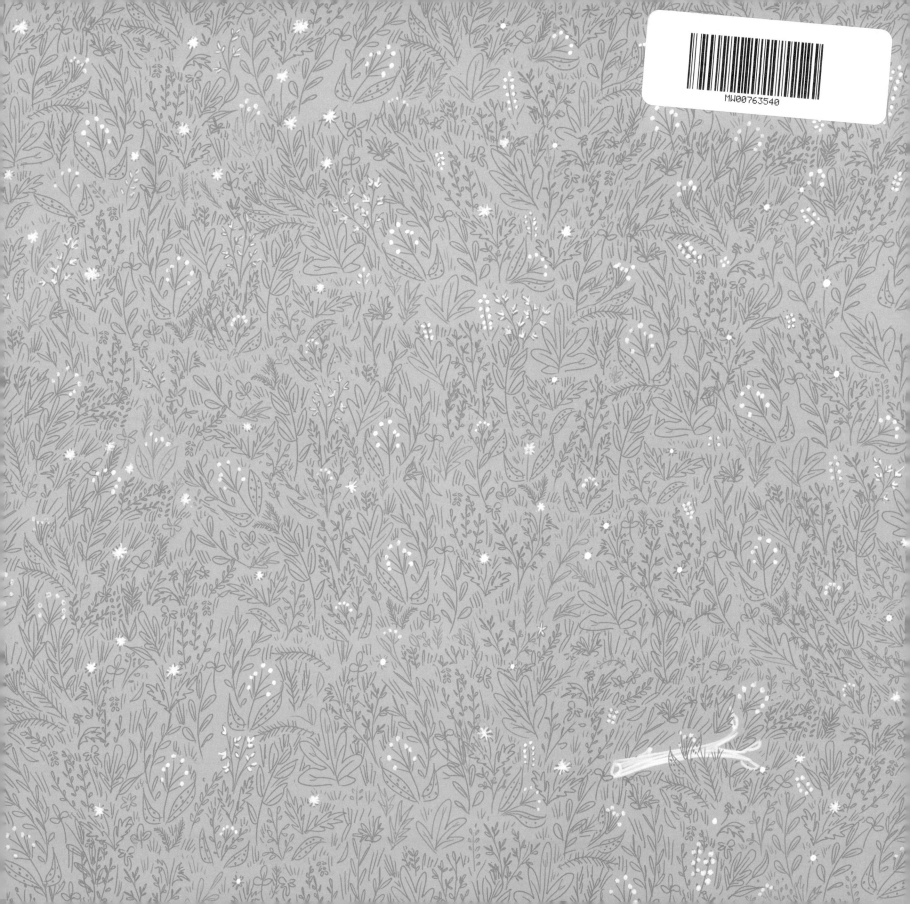

MW00763540

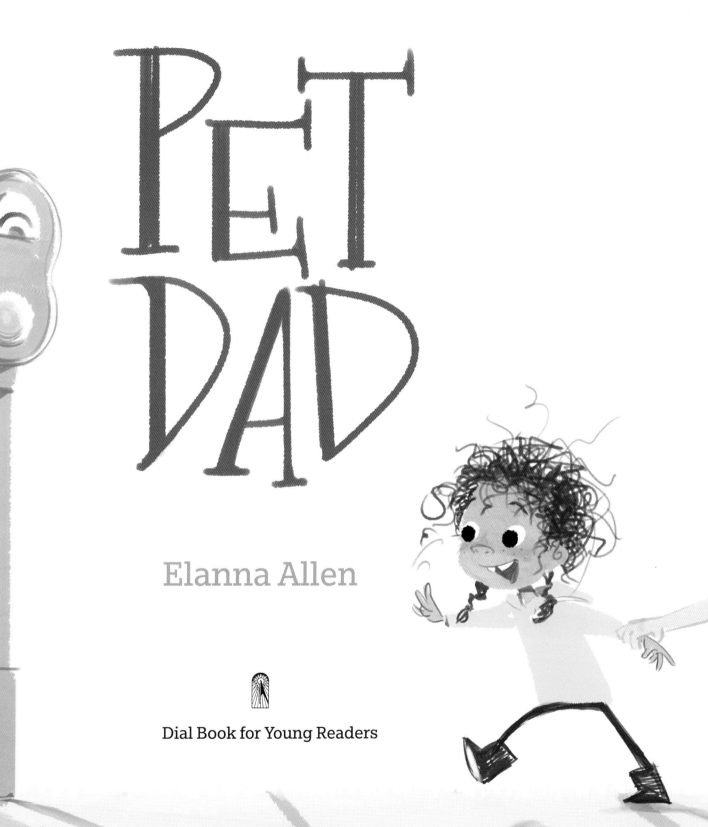

PET DAD

Elanna Allen

Dial Book for Young Readers

Dial Books for Young Readers
Penguin Young Readers Group
An imprint of Penguin Random House LLC
375 Hudson Street, New York, NY 10014

Copyright © 2018 Elanna Allen

Penguin supports copyright. Copyright fuels creativity,
encourages diverse voices, promotes free speech, and creates
a vibrant culture. Thank you for buying an authorized edition
of this book and for complying with copyright laws by not
reproducing, scanning, or distributing any part of it in any form
without permission. You are supporting writers and allowing
Penguin to continue to publish books for every reader.

Printed in China
ISBN 9780525428268
2 3 4 5 6 7 8 9 10

Design by Lily Malcom
Text set in Egyptian Slate Pro and hand lettered by the artist.
The art was created with pencil and ink with digital color.

For Nico, Sebastian, and their pet dad, Andreas.

Woof.

Plum wants a

Plum's dad does *not* want a pet.

Specifically, he wants

NO

pet.

So Plum,
who never takes

NO

for an answer,

gets herself the only pet she can.

A pet dad.

With a little training, Plum knows that she and her new pet will enjoy many years of friendship.

And she might not need a leash, a muzzle, or even that cone thing.

Plum adores her new pet.

She rubs his tummy.

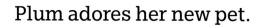

She scratches
behind his ears.

She names him

SCHNITZEL!

But when it comes to caring for Schnitzel,
Plum runs into a spot of trouble.

First she must feed her pet.
Plum knows that pet grown-ups eat
disgusting foods, like kale and quinoa.
In a pinch, yard waste will do.

But when Plum tries to feed this mess
to her pet, he barks

NO.

Schnitzel has a
different way to eat.

Next Plum must teach her pet when and where to do his business.

But when she tries to paper-train her pet, again he barks

NO!

Schnitzel has a different use for the newspaper.

That night, Plum tries to sleep-train her pet. Again with the

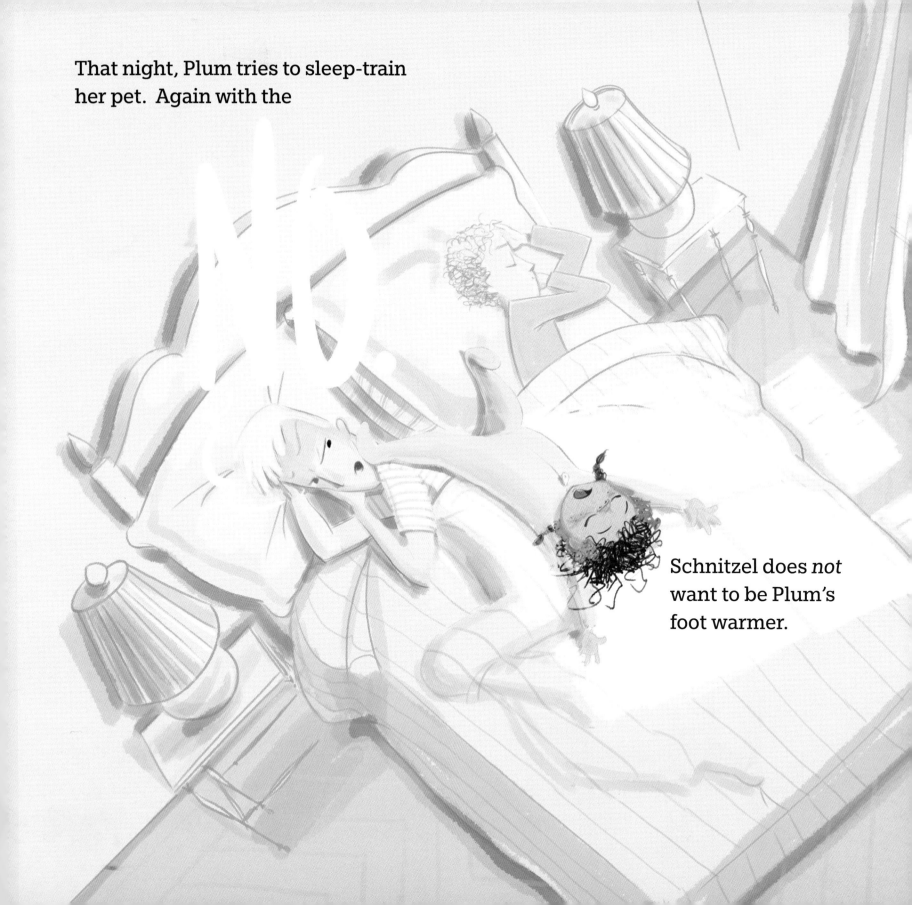

Schnitzel does *not* want to be Plum's foot warmer.

It isn't easy caring for a pet.
Especially a pet grown-up.

The next morning, rested and refreshed, Plum takes her pet to the park to teach him some new tricks.

She trains Schnitzel to

SiT!

HECK NO,

he barks.

She trains him to FETCH!!

Then she trains Schnitzel to

CHASE!!!

That works a little better,

until Schnitzel starts barking loudly.

GET BACK HERE!!!

Very loudly.

Plum knows
she has to be firm.

Or not.

With some unexpected free time,
Plum sits down for a good think.
This pet training is *not* going well.

The missing piece, Plum reasons, is a *reward* for her pet.
But what is a good reward?

What does Plum have that pet dads
love *most* of all?

And then she has a stroke of genius!

NO + HUG

= YES!

The hug—a perfect reward for a pet dad.

With her recent success, Plum tries the math again.

PLEASE + HUG = ICE CREAM

Next she discovers

SiT + HUG = PiCNiC

And finally, ROLL OVER + HUG = PLAYTIME!

And from that day forward, Plum and her pet
enjoy many years of friendship and love.

And she never needs a leash,
a muzzle, or even that cone thing.

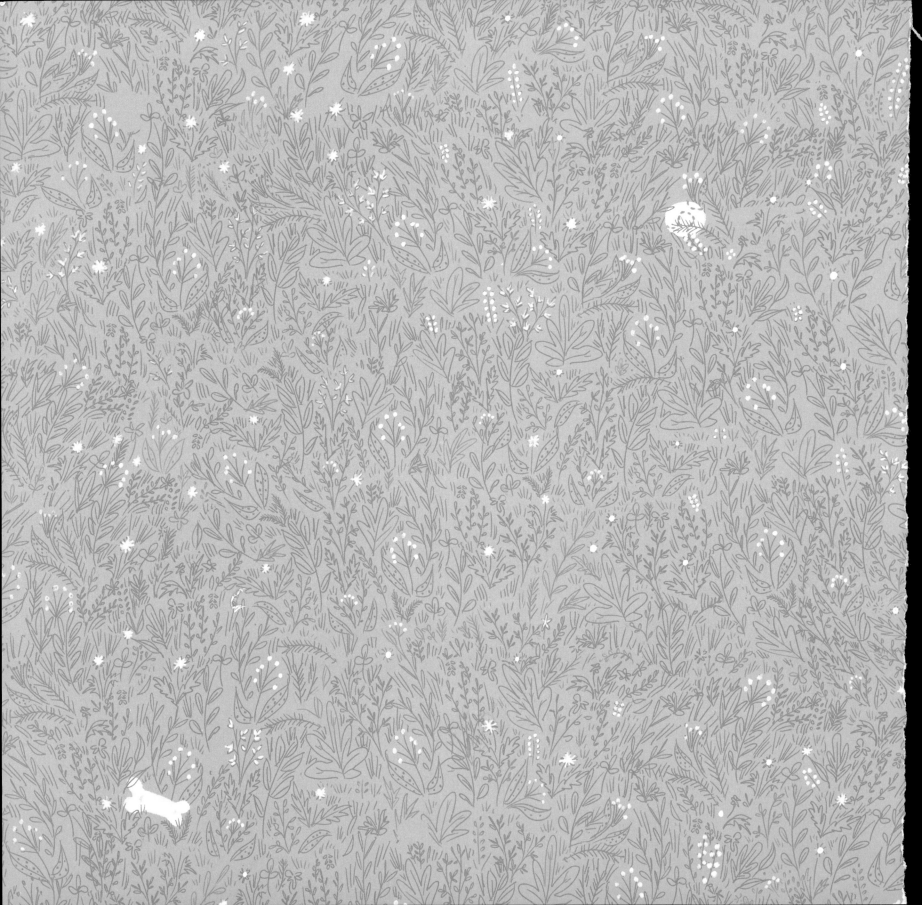